Dinnertime!

By **Sue Williams**

Illustrated by **Kerry Argent**

HARCOURT, INC.

San Diego   New York   London

Printed in Singapore

Six fat rabbits, doing what they please,
don't see the fox sneak out of the trees.

Run, fat rabbits! Run, run, run!
That fox wants to eat you, one by one!

Dinnertime!

Five fat rabbits, climbing up to play,
don't see the fox hiding in the hay.

Run, fat rabbits! Run, run, run!
That fox wants to eat you,
one by one!

Dinnertime!

Four fat rabbits, leaping all around,
don't see the fox jump up from the ground.

Run, fat rabbits! Run, run, run!
That fox wants to eat you, one by one!

Dinnertime!

Three fat rabbits, away from their burrow,
don't see the fox spring up from a furrow.

Run, fat rabbits! Run, run, run!
That fox wants to eat you,
one by one!

Two fat rabbits, playing hide-and-seek, don't see the fox pretending he's asleep.

Run, fat rabbits! Run, run, run!
That fox wants to eat you, one by one!

Dinnertime!

One fat rabbit, all on its own,
out in the dark, a long way from home.

Run, fat rabbit! Run, run, run!
That fox wants to eat you, little one!

Dinnertime!

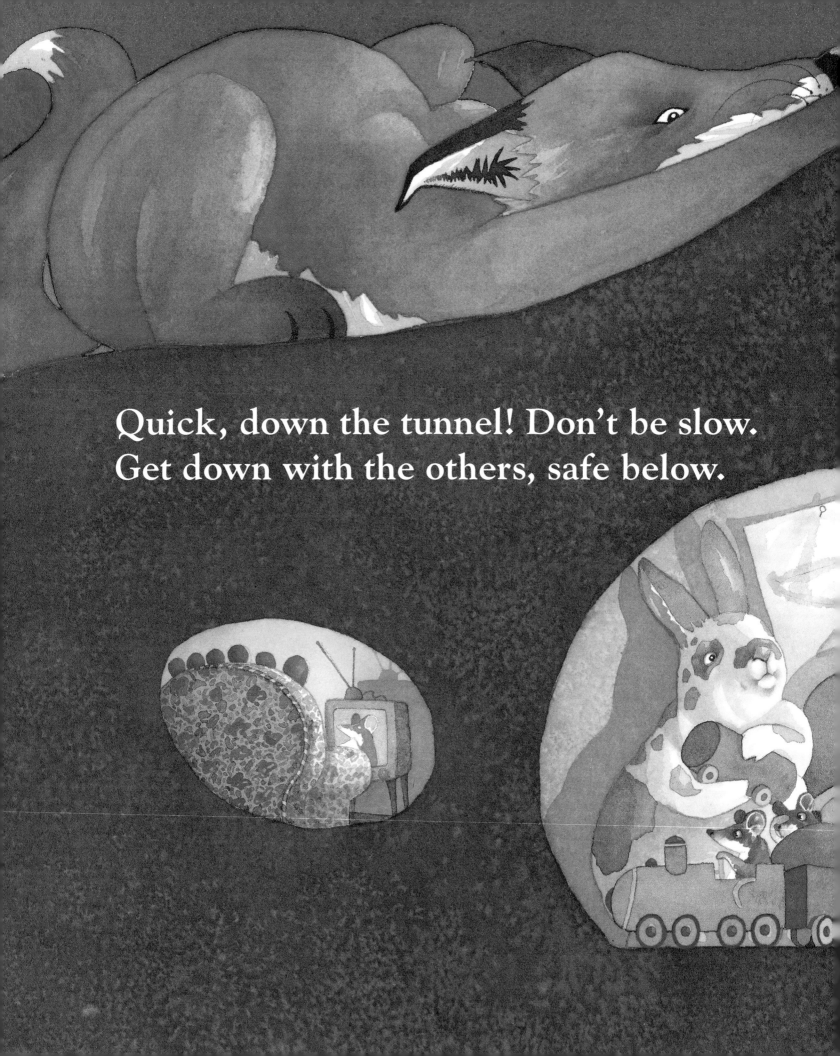

Quick, down the tunnel! Don't be slow.
Get down with the others, safe below.

Six fat rabbits, eating cabbage rolls,
listen as their mother scolds:

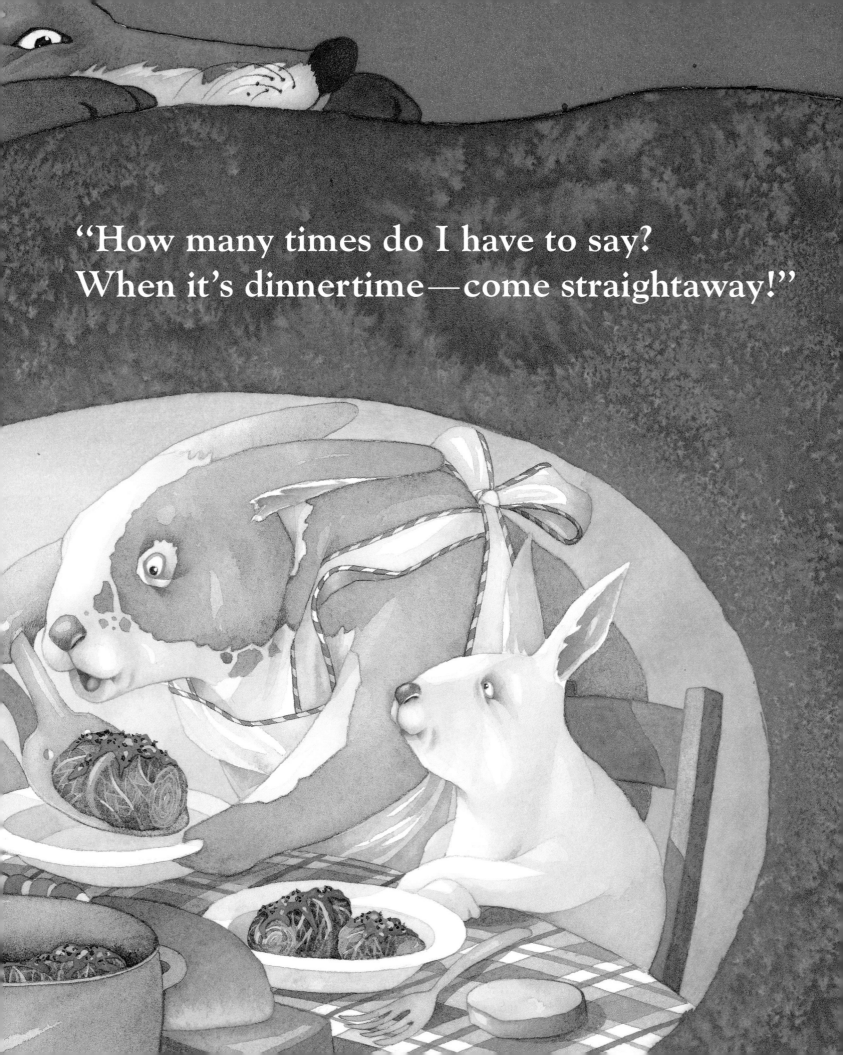

"How many times do I have to say?
When it's dinnertime—come straightaway!"

www.harcourt.com

First published in Australia in 2001 by Working Title Press
First U.S. edition 2002

Library of Congress Cataloging-in-Publication Data
Williams, Sue, 1948–
Dinnertime!/Sue Williams; illustrated by Kerry Argent.
p.   cm.
Summary: One by one, six little rabbits escape a hungry fox.
[1. Rabbits—Fiction.   2. Foxes—Fiction.   3. Counting.   4. Stories in rhyme.]
I. Argent, Kerry, 1960– ill.   II. Title.
PZ8.3.W67927Di   2002
[E]—dc21   2001001956
ISBN 0-15-216471-5

C E G H F D B

The illustrations in this book were done in watercolor.
The display type was set in Humana Serif Medium.
The text type was set in Goudy Catalogue.
U.S. edition designed by Judythe Sieck